DAISY
You Do!

To Dennis, Nancy, Liberty and Phoebe – K.G.
For Jessica and Emily – N.S.

DAISY: YOU DO!
A RED FOX BOOK 978 1 782 95648 8
First published in Great Britain by The Bodley Head, an imprint of Random House Children's Publishers UK
A Penguin Random House Company

The Bodley Head edition published 2003
Red Fox edition published 2004
This edition published 2016

1 3 5 7 9 10 8 6 4 2

Text copyright © Kes Gray, 2003
Illustrations copyright © Nick Sharratt, 2003

Penguin Random House is committed to a sustainable future for our business, our readers and our planet.
This book is made from Forest Stewardship Council® certified paper.

MIX
Paper from
responsible sources
FSC® C018179

Red Fox Books are published by Random House Children's Publishers UK,
61–63 Uxbridge Road, London W5 5SA

www.randomhousechildrens.co.uk www.randomhouse.co.uk

Addresses for companies within The Random House Group Limited can be found at: www.randomhouse.co.uk/offices.htm

THE RANDOM HOUSE GROUP Limited Reg. No. 954009

A CIP catalogue record for this book is available from the British Library.

Printed in China

DAISY
You Do!

Kes Gray & Nick Sharratt

RED FOX

"Don't pick your nose,"
said Daisy's *mum.*
"You do," said Daisy.
"When?" said Daisy's *mum.*
"In the car on the way
to Nanny's," said Daisy.
"I wasn't picking,
I was scratching,"
explained Daisy's *mum.*

"Don't slurp your soup," said Daisy's *mum*.

"You do," said Daisy.

"When?" said Daisy's *mum*.

"On Saturday when we had chicken noodle," said Daisy.

"That's because I'd been to the dentist,"

explained Daisy's *mum*.

"Don't leave your clothes on the floor," said Daisy's *mum*.

"You do," said Daisy.

"When?" said Daisy's *mum*.

"Last week when you were going to that party," said Daisy.

"I couldn't decide what to wear," explained Daisy's *mum*.

"Don't wear your wellies in the house," said Daisy's *mum*.

"You do," said Daisy.

"When?" said Daisy's *mum*.

"Last weekend when you came in from the garden," said Daisy.

"That's because I had to fill the watering can," explained Daisy's *mum*.

"Don't keep fidgeting," said Daisy's *mum*.

"You do," said Daisy.

"When?" said Daisy's *mum*.

"In the church at that wedding we went to," said Daisy.

"That's because the seats were too hard," explained Daisy's *mum*.

"Don't sit so close to the telly," said Daisy's *mum*.

"You do," said Daisy.

"When?" said Daisy's *mum*.

"When you were watching that soppy film," said Daisy. "I didn't have *my* contact lenses in," explained Daisy's *mum*.

"Don't talk with your mouth full," said Daisy's *mum*.

"You do," said Daisy.

"When?" said Daisy's *mum*.

"When your jacket potato was too hot," said Daisy.

"I wasn't talking, I was blowing,"

explained Daisy's *mum*.

"Don't lollop," said Daisy's *mum*.

"You do," said Daisy.

"When?" said Daisy's *mum*.

"Last Monday evening," said Daisy.

"I'd just done my exercises,"
explained Daisy's *mum*.

"Don't eat all the nice ones," said Daisy's *mum*.

"You do," said Daisy.

"When?" said Daisy's *mum*.

"All the time," said Daisy.

"That's because I only like the nice ones,"
explained Daisy's *mum*.

"Don't keep saying '**you do**'," said Daisy's *mum*.

"You do," chuckled Daisy.

Daisy's *mum* put her hands on her hips and looked Daisy straight in the eye.
"I do not keep saying 'you do', **YOU DO!**"

"You just said it **TWICE!**" giggled Daisy.

"Right, who deserves a good tickling?" laughed Daisy's *mum*, chasing Daisy into the garden.

"I DO! I DO!"
squealed Daisy.

DAISY

LITTLE TROUBLE

**There are many more
Daisy picture books to discover:**

- Daisy: 006 and a Bit
- Daisy: Eat Your Peas
- Daisy: Tiger Ways
- Daisy: Really, Really
- Daisy: Yuk!
- Super Daisy

BIG TROUBLE

**Join Daisy on these
adventures for older readers:**

- Daisy and the Trouble with Giants
- Daisy and the Trouble with Kittens
- Daisy and the Trouble with Life
- Daisy and the Trouble with Zoos

. . . AND MANY MORE!